radical madness

radical madness

albert klassen

radical madness

Publisher: DEE ELL PUBLISHING

ISBN: 978-0-9812123-6-4

Further information: albertklassen@icloud.com

Books by Albert Klassen

the death of the girl with the beautiful hair
looking at life from an angle
the life of lido pepperman
the church
radical madness
a monk in paradise
the abstract god
journey
never been to berlin

Chapter One

he walked carelessly across the tracks
eating snacks
a wandering minstrel upset and carrying on
asking silly questions about life

oh the news
I'm not winning anymore and hey you joe
what can you do
the lies grow on the yellow snow as beatlejuice jumps
and that hair
messy

all those diamonds falling from the sky
oh me oh my
baby don't be shy

and please - don't say goodbye

no strings
I want to know the location of the station
are there fat generals on parade
is it a charade
with no one making the grade

hey you
what can you do
the lies grew
as the stork flew

it seemed so long ago but it was only yesterday when
I saw the shadows
the music is just reaching my soul now
aching with pain and nostalgic paranoia I groan
please release me
please rehearse me
please take these monsters away from my house

who can last
thundering hooves
accordion player alone in the corner in the basement
the L.P. is playing on the turntable
changing tunes they are whistling
boys please quit dancing on the roof of the bus
a yellow bus
she didn't cave as he flinched in the club and Alice
flicked her butt at the bartender

take that stupid guy
everything is going to hell on earth
can't you see and feel the power like an abomination

god is going to get mad again and
what are you trying to prove

war is coming in time with the marching boots
anyone up to speed
crash de de boom boom
eliza on the head
ouch
it's like falling into a sewer
or love
is there a difference
spike the punch and raise the stakes
times are strange
out here on the range

the end is near he shouted as he dragged a cross
across the intersection
worship the lamb of god
accept his blood atonement
and all the people shouted
but the dogs still barked at the monument
and pissed upon the broken glass scattered

the world is a big big place
lots of space
mountains and valleys

cities
shitholes and losers that want to destroy and
annihilate you
debutantes with big baggy trousers peeking in at
windows and drinking
peach schnapps

the giant forests cover giant swaths of the land
many animals and insects and diseases
frogs too trying to survive
we all want to survive
and thrive
and so we connive

I stood at the edge and protested
I want to die
why the hell do I keep on living
for what purpose
this broken road
an apocalyptic nightmare
insulted daily and forced to be a slave
a knave
I want to go and live in a cave
and study and sing
a solitary man
alone
no problems - PEACE

I am a man but
men are barbarians except for

me
I'm civilized
women need to rule the world and
us apes need to be chained up
so many motherfuckers
makes me sick
and who are we all
nobody perhaps
what is civilization
do we know or understand

I watch as the leaven rises the bread
as in ancient days
those days of yore
the pain of the past rises also
and I try to subdue the memories

sometimes we plead and beg
on our knees
blinded by
our rage
our pain
our helplessness
and we crouch in terror wondering
is survival a possibility

the judgements come down
everyone has become a judge
condemning is a national pastime
violence everywhere

we are animals
dam savage beasts

is the world an act of faith on god's part
does god trust in
our righteousness

walking on this lonely road
watch out for the bandits
but in the end
an image of the docile female
marching along behind her man
will be gone forever
call it evolution
or just desserts

we heard that the lord is our shepard
and even though we walk through the valley of evil
and in the shadow of death
we need not fear for god is there
almighty god we need you
even though you are a mystery
who are you
what do you think
we walk by faith
not by sight

directionless and aimless
driving in circles
what were the councillors recommendations

the collectors anxiety fumbled the ball at the wrong
moment
historically significant moments left unrecorded lest
anyone place the blame

I really hate the endless rain because
it made me feel so down and depressed
everyone was out of sorts and when that happens
the spirits
dampened
not uplifted
and then when we get a sunny day we don't know
what to do about it
so we wander around and mutter - nice day eh
nice day for sure man
we're retarded for sure

I slept for days in my bed
why get up
for whatever

in what land do you live
and does it matter
rituals are everywhere even if we don't recognize their
importance
playing with hallucinations
interpreting dreams
having exotic and passionate sex - also so disturbing

the neutrality of token symbols must be emphasized

and the relics
they all evolved as our artists gave substance to the
dreams of the many
comical expressionism defining the problems

being fascists in one form or another is an abstract
form of anger

the teacher tied andy to a chair and whipped him
with a nylon rope
andy shrieked as the other pupils cheered the teacher
on
whip him good
whip him hard
whip him till his blood runs on the floor
whip him till he dies
the students cheered and cheered
but the teacher stopped and untied andy who ran
away screaming

out of his cave the monk peered
what's going on out there - wait don't tell me and
please bring me food and water
the people stared as the monk glared
they brought him food and water
now I can continue to study and pray to God for all
of you he said
the people thanked him
andy was a holy man and also crazy
crazy as a bat - but respected by the masses

roll away the stone

obscene is the craft of the priests - perverts
pretending to serve god
their self-importance and fake humility builds up the
ego
self-destructive forces within us drag us into the
gutter where in the shade of demonic trees we rot
and smell
horned toads and witchy women are collaborating
with sick musicians to deprive us of a reasonable
chance at decency and honour
our future compromised and economized - doesn't
exist anymore

historically our fanaticism was a saving grace that
saved us from the coming machine age
morality was invented by immoral men so they
could by subversion and compromise seduce and
manipulate and control mankind
god is watching in horror

the fisherman screamed out into the storm - where is
the righteous path
is that furious anger from a vengeful god
has god been crossed or doublecrossed

the world is turning
away
the moon is sighing

under the lights the mothers are crying
even the popular kids are getting lonely clinking
glasses together
down in the basement of the church

tears amidst the jeers
will I be alright
just don't know anymore and hope
it'll only get you so far
is there a comeback in the cards
the jester is shuffling
along the street
and to the beat the cop
is tapping his baton
is there room for a broken dreamer

why not a big solid wall for protection
don't people want to be safe anymore
you want these strangers killing you in your own
home and
taking your money and your pride and your life and
come on what's going on
banging heads on poles
nobody scoring any goals
everybody digging holes

universal standards of behaviour are there
ignored by irreverent religions and their leaders
punishment must be meted out proportionally
or anarchy

no rules
no protocols
no principles

banning sex was a start
covering up women was the pretext for curbing the
anxiety among men
central to a proper absolute mandate
combatting the madness
this uncertainty meets that compulsion
explosions in the belfry
ring the bells and send the message
peeling
as if the oranges were rotten and the eaters morally
decadent
ripping up the codes of conduct as without a
compass
all cultures remaining indifferent to universal values

in communism we will find our answer
the world is a giant commune
all things held in common as in the early church
universal healthcare
shared highways and public buildings
by the people and
for the people as we do it together and share the risk
we're communists
democracy is communism
who are we kidding anyways
society means communism

communal and shared

the tendency towards refinement must be faught
everything must be polished
and distorted and pulled apart and reexamined and
closely scrutinized
perhaps there is a decadent dogma inherent in the
painting and
if we look we will become negatively influenced and
become losers
in a natural light exposed our narcissism
as organically we compose a version of reality that
confuses

the little baker on the corner was infatuated by
metaphysical elements
take a little dough
mix in some personal feelings
mix it some more
then let the influence of fashion turn it into a work
of delight
yum yum
herr baker you are a genius

on the main street where the protestors and police
clash
the lone violinist plays on unperturbed
they rip the violin from his hands
only then the music stops
it's a metaphor for the world

we all play on but soon
our broken violins will float in a sea of blood
our own
will then the music stop

machines eye us without blinking
what could they be thinking
nothing except an extension of thoughts percolating
they command under command
steadfast in their commitment
an orderly existence

sir marx and lord lenin had a vision
of course they had a vision
a plan
however they misjudged the character of mankind
the proposals didn't work in their particular
environment but with a tweet here and there
perhaps we can give it another go
or

martha was barbecuing and the sauce
decadent and hearty
at the other end of town the losers were gathering
and making eye contact with
slutty veronica who was wearing those short shorts
what's up girl
gonna drag all those men into the gutter
nevertheless come sunday pastor hank will preach the
word

totally oblivious
tis wonderful to live in a bubble
ignorance is bliss
that kiss and
tell me please was it good for you
or you
avoiding the conversations
as we dwell in the past
the momentum continues
who's to blame
again the beurocrats
nasty rats
how do they sleep at night unburdened by their lack
of compassion
unruffled by the human misery
stand back
agony not shared or cared for
sensing and drinking with the tattoo artist
right there mister

happy dragons
massacred villagers gasping
breath is scarce
will anyone say that they are sorry
oh sorry
we so need the almighty - is there another way
calm down please
the world is a disaster and the pool - cold
still
underlying reasons are pulling my leg

the cause
we embellish as thoughts cross
and the big red bows
look nice

Chapter Two

within the echo
desperation
the angry mob is tired
the missing respect chasing a fantasy
requirements of substance create avenues of disquiet
deep-seated misery clashes with haunting melodies
guidenceless fear
all those scapegoats lining up at the office and
holding out their hands

play the sonata by mozart again
and at the coffee shop
where sam implored his friends to tone it down
they laughed

cheese with that
always something else to compliment
god save the king
mary mary quite contrary
the peas in the garden
growing and
there will be a tasty treat

then the big explosion
outside my window
angels blowing up a heavenly bomb

a hat and sunglasses
was it a disguise
or god
blackmailing his own creation
nailing up the indulgences on the cross
calvary was the conference centre
planning judgement

it was a coverup
god washing his hands with blood
even lucifer was fooled
but now
time to play avenger
but it all bombed in the end
such a shame
all those threats
just a game
and so much collateral damage

the ether is the grid that connects it all
gravity the force
the machine controls
a soulless instrument
it was programmed by its creators to create a creature
with a soul
connecting the dots of the ether with gravity

the spiral of eternity
from nothing out to everything and then
back to the proverbial point and then - nothing - and
then
spiralling outward again
god is the machine

government has become a colossal failure
we have become it's servants
not the other way around
it has a fence around it and only lets in dubious
individuals
those with stones for hearts and greed
mount thy steed
oh Isabella and do not cede
thy power lest the slaves are freed
and change the intent of the ruling creed
oh lady that would be a dastardly deed
especially after all that weed
was smoked and the king refused to heed
the peasants message and refused to lead
the masses who were teed

off and complaining about the need
for the fairness for which they plead

anyways it's all gone to pot
and the world is in chaos as jumping jack flash
is waving around a lot of cash
and demanding a place at the table
to discuss
what
new knickers and more male whores

I simply can't look anymore
the alpha and omega are prancing around the table
you first
no you
it never ends and that's why eternity
is such a valuable commodity
buyers beware though
with no end in sight new problems are bound to arise

to the library to get a book
to the kitchen to try to cook
to the riot to take a look

a pick axe is necessary
or an oliver cromwell
the masses must be controlled
manipulated
even plato wanted that
and the guillotine

those savage hearts
so untamed and fierce
raving lunatics
walking on the strasse with their poodles
in circles
like insane nuts
watching the bullies creeping into the square
their faces grinning
the moonlight
shining
on their faces and
in the background the pied piper
turning into a vampire
a bloody mess like the crucifixion

oh I get it now my friend
as I'm standing in the sunlight at the entrance to the
park
gravity is not to be understood since
einstein muddied the waters with his slipshod
theorizing and
conjecture
well - goes to show how naive we all are
infatuated with nonsense
throw the dart
where did it land

seeking after salvation to attain the ultimate
harmony
please affirm the divine intention

let the interns join hands and pray
are you objective as you seek your own divine order
the degenerates are riding their bikes and praying
for insight even as they call themselves atheists
mysteriously vanishing into the classrooms and
cursing all gods everywhere
a new religion for a brand new day
I saw it in a revelation
on blackboards of despair and loathing it was written
and witnessed by the revival experts
one and two and three
presto you are free
sinless and benign - the scriptures confirming your
conversion
and in heaven your name is written in the book
so stop all that worrying
heaven awaits
are you faithful
and can you read the expression on the face of god
who's hiding in the shadows and spying on you
do this
don't do that
aha caught you

revellers rampaging and getting strung out
ring the bells
sound the alarm
rally the troops

the sailer walked around the square

trinkets anyone
trinkets for free
who loves nice jangled trinkets
a trinket for an acre of land seemed to be a fair deal
and
throw in a warm jacket

a racist was walking down the road one day
she was naked and happy and gay
singing psalms and finding her way
to the church to pray
the priest was appalled as she made her way in
he shouted you are full of sin
and took her into a prayer bin
had sex and drank some gin

thou shalt not frown upon those who make less
money than you
riches entitles the owner to be superior
do this
do that
slaves abound
franky found a lot of money in a dumpster and was
happy as could be
went out and bought a new car
drove around and acted like a jerk
look at me I'm rich
hey bitch
be my slave
you got the money

I got the time
the picture was all wrong with discriminatory
undertones
this society is kaput

coffee donuts espresso sandwiches latte bagels
the big round belly was uncomfortable for the fat
man
another muffin please
beer and swiss fries for breakfast

eating till our stomachs burst
like our pride
or a tractor ploughing the neighbours field
under

these holy men all puffed up
we know it's all shady
power-seeking and full of
it
sick of it
and
have we no brains at all
or did we contract a disease
leave it all alone and why not end the charade
no more thou shalt not
no more and the lord said
no more peeing in the pickle jar
come on already
grow a pair

john said as soon as you're born they make you feel
small
who are you then
the cops arrest you for nothing
and big brother watches so he can throw you into
prison
we must be more important than anyone else
with more power and
influence
and of course we must pretend to care

old Saint Nick was a merry soul
or so they say
as for myself I enjoy a good muffin with a cup of tea
and then sit in the hot tub with a group of drunks
all pissing and pissed
shouting and laughing
we forget the world and love ourselves

I do is not for the faint of heart
a lifetime commitment made while still young and
dumb
do you love me
yes of course
wink wink
and then as life unfolds some poor souls lose heart
they go mad and drown their sorrow in pills and
bottles
how can I go on

for god so loved the world that he destroyed almost
everyone and everything
in the flood
that was not a good thing people
thank god it was a myth

the world is a barbaric place
I want to hide in my room and never
come out again
they're cutting people's heads off and
torturing children and women
I can't stand the pain of thinking about it
I want to be an ostrich
why do our leaders sit on their hands and play coy
why the inaction
why playing only lip service
to the depths I go
to Hades I wander
my spirit is dead and I
dread this cold cold winter
recovery is impossible and my mission will be
aborted
woe is me and humanity
the poison of brutal religiosity is killing us
our refuge is gone

the hunter was lost in the deep woods
calling out loudly
my companions where are you
friends please hear me and come

an imminent rescue would suit the situation
the wolves were howling as the hunter became
the hunted
darkness fell and the eyes shone yellow in the full
moon
he shot at them
they cried out as dying some fell and then the rest
ran away
safe and alone and praying for
daylight
oh
there you are

the mind confused and tired
cries out for relief
spending time amidst the ruins of yesterday
a comfort noble and
detached
we touch the rubble as the rain
washes away the ashes
as whitewashed the skeletons shine
a reflection of postmodern blues

can a brand new day be around the corner
who can you trust
survivors guilt
our neverending road to
tragedy
and freedom
behind those bars of steel

blessed be the seekers

this sublime posture
laying prostrate on the ground
in touch with the demons that ravage and seduce the
troubled soul
as a crisis of spiritual depravity grows among
followers of the natural
order
and
can this sanction of national appetites survive
destroyed and annihilated and forgotten
the remains stolen
throw away the key
nothing will be the new password
emptiness
spaceless space
baseless base
caseless case
with not a thing explained
Alice please shut the door for the enlightenment was
only a distraction

peeking into a stained glass ball
roy wood singing see my baby jive
a prophet truly
and the costumes perhaps
reflective of a deeper vision of God
gravitational ethereal communication beyond
senses that seem to be restrained or wild

the musician was keen
to buy a pair of blue jean-
s and be seen
with clara the queen
of mean
after all he was just a teen
and had just been
working out so he could be lean
and also - his name was dean

the take away was far from ordered or even clear
as the tears that were shed didn't appear
to be real so please dear
greta try a little tenderness on this night of evil
intentions
because greatness is not even a consideration
even as the five men riding their bicycles
are smoking cigars and drinking beer
so much for sobriety and order
in circles going
and look - mad people everywhere going in circles
around
and around
dizzy with an unfinished manuscript that doesn't
even make sense
repaint the scenes and give the keys to the apprentice

stacking red blocks
the wall was getting higher
then it stopped and

a helicopter dropped a line
down and
a naked woman came down and
sat on the wall
a bullhorn in her hand
I am the daughter of god
I will free you from your sin
come and kiss my feet
experience the love and forgiveness
a skeptical mankind ran away with hands
over ears
it was a sunny day with a band playing
so the people danced

let me ask
what if
the Beatles never existed as a band
or Jesus had died in childbirth
or Hitler had never been born
what then

Chapter Three

the sidewalks are full of bums with cardboard signs
give me some money man
jingle jangle

the drip drip drip of the water in the night
the boom boom boom of the neighbours bass in the
music
the caw caw caw of the complaining crows

horas - mithras - jesus
this story we have heard before
history is so muddied and the voices
the ancient testimonies
fabrications
the foundations of our faith and our truth

walking on eggshells
trample not upon my beliefs lest I cut thee asunder
sacred and holy is the ground I tremble upon
curses befall the doubting mind

sedation in the black hole
paper masks over the isolated faces
everything is over now mr.cool
silent screaming after
all that
scheming
now the spacecraft is taking new passengers and
outer space is calling
the interest in moon technology fuelled the passion
somewhere is coming into view as flying
the loneliness
an ice cream from dairy queen would be really nice
right now
we heard him say

will you audition for the role of the killer in the new
quentin movie
you're gonna need a long sword
and boxers
and you gotta be female
hope you can dance
or prance
or be up for some romance

man sits beside musician eating a banana

man says yummy
man falls off piano bench
musician laughs
who wants to live forever
anyways

broken pieces are flying off the moon
gifts given to the aliens
part of the great intergalactic family
connected by the essence
life
united within the ether
forever inseparable
children touching each other over the distances
without knowing
a universe together and part of god
blindly we go where our dreams haven't even found a
foothold
extraterrestrials we are to someone
somewhere

queen fernandona loved her castle of steel as
the ufo's were flying past her kitchen window
open up the morning paper - it's there for all to see
and the price
following the latest craze
take out your own bath water but when it comes to
blowing out your brains
allow the courtier
and the natives

jumping off cliffs and swearing that there's life on
other planets
of course
factor in the scientific theories unproven
acceptable nonetheless because the stone was rolled
away
two thousand years ago
as the kingdoms of this world compete with the
spirit of
darkness as the end of the age
broken but replaced maybe
existentialism is triggered by the faith in the twisted
images of peace
but the war was reported to have opened up on two
fronts with
beth clinging to a rock in the middle of the river
Euphrates
she had eaten out of goblets of titanium
screeching brakes - hey you and a pound of flesh
turbulent discourses and the clip clop of hooves as
the messenger is arriving with news and the hair is let
down
on the corner with the children of slums and rulers
of pergatory
drowning in the sorrow of a godless reality so bother
reach out acting
the dispute was featuring as the hardened hearts
would not yield
I fear the end
why can we not mend

and all the cash we spend
bring the bottle

there are three ways
in addition to all the rest and can we reason together
in this hall of mirrors
the five classics caught our collective attention as
servants
embracing a rearrangement of the
internal
the purification was in jeopardy but nothing
happened to apprehend all the thieves
let's break the bread together then
pass the wine
only when we are drunk will we see eye to eye and
shut the dam gate to the vineyard

lucy stood up at the meeting and rebuked the elders
how dare you sinful yaks proceed with a heavenly
mandate
it is written
shot down this unholy war with the transvestites
new rites
are needed as the temple is burning
even as our stomachs are churning
don't blame all the harlots
they lie in pain at the temple gates with knives in
their backs
then all the liars stood up and fled
death do not call my number even though

the band is playing my song
it won't be long
let me be strong
were we all so wrong

I watched as a basket of flowers descended from
heaven accompanied
by celestial music
the priest stood up in his white robes
blessed is the synagogue for in it we see god
revealed as all the stupid men and wise women
colluded and planned
a feast to commemorate a brutal history
magnificence
we are all
children of the sky
so why
do we die
and hope that some fry

all those covenants were so imaginary don't
the leaders understand
shedding the blood was nonsensical and
so barbarian and still
our will
is weak even as our gullibility is strong and
the creature slithered along the grass looking for prey
over the mountains and through the ages the chariots
moved
breakneck speed

scrolls of religious bullshit raining down from the
sky upon
this unsuspecting generation as defying and
glorifying
reach out and forsake the tradition
save yourself

why is the violin out of tune and the bassoon so loud
we need the spice
and some flavour to make things seem righteous and
important
sit upon those pillars and don't laugh
ha ha - trapped we are
a pitiful bunch
kabbalah indeed
secret doctrines undermined reality and even as they
pranced
and danced in the hearts of immoral men
the children of earth multiplied

the wolf was reincarnated from a dove
peace could not keep pace with the gods of war
hey emperor stay in your castle lest I slay you
dismembered thou shalt be
cast upon the rocks while thy flesh be picked by
eagles and degenerates
oh mary full of grace release us
the rosary
the bag of tricks
and smelly old dicks

break the sticks
and return our nobility that was stolen

coats with many colours were
hanging next to the bookshelves where
books of lenin and confuscious
gathered dust

don't take me to the forest
dark and dank it scares me
no freedom in its shade
only terror and death
those trees are conspiring
cut them all down and allow
the sun to shine and watch
satan run to the caves to drink his whiskey and gin
indulging in all his sin
away from the din
of gods people's chatter

profits before prayer
greenbacks rain down like nuclear fallout upon the
poor who reaching up
collapse as the power breaks upon them
a nasty dose of despair
run and hide and let not the masters see your desire
or ambition
naked and pretentious all at the same time
lord have mercy as struggling along
highways of despair amidst the back alleys of

opulence
a cascading waterfall of decadence cloaked in a
pretence of goodness
the wholesome hypocrisy

all the slumlords please stand up and come and get
your medals
praise to you for taking advantage of the poor and
needy
and lining your pockets with their hard earned money
kudos for being thieves and robbers
enabled by lawyers judges and politicians
dirty swine together sniffing and snorting caca
for taking the bread from the children of the
disenfranchised
building your castles and buying fancy cars
you cream of the crop
you wonderful kind and loving masters
you rotten deprived monsters

you raped us and pillaged
our women you debased
our children you bullied and beat
you murdered our innocence
in your beds snakes will crawl
you subverters of order and righteousness
you fake and dishonest promoters of hate violence
and immorality
you took all the power and
disrespected us

you nailed us to crosses and despised and rejected us
and killed us

the mademoiselle looked demure in her long fox fur
coat
she sauntered up the street to the beat
of the beach boys song - God only knows
oblivious to the stares
and glares
she held her head high and smiled provocatively
and from an apartment on the seventh floor of a
neighbouring highrise
an elderly man lusted
and thought of the old days
ah-h-h he sighed
those were the days
the innocence and
the joy

ripping out pages of the latest vogue - the painter
considered a motif
the painting should be
alive with colours and still confusing
can I interest you in a bagel with cream cheese and
lox and capers
or maybe a slab of bacon

streams of consciousness together gasp
then scream
again

I'm still thinking about the burning bush and
well could it have been only an illusion
or made up
never have we seen it again
and remember it talked
well not it exactly but a voice came out of it
could a loudspeaker have been hidden near it and
fooled Moses
sorry that had not been invented yet
my point exactly
we wait for evolution as we dream
this
then that

what if we burned all the bibles

bitterness is inevitable
what choice is there when down down down
you go
nothing makes sense anymore and even the natural
rhythm
interrupted
nightmares they come and snatch your rest
death is a great art form
on this canvass of despair we witness the greatest
pieces

revenge my dear she said
and at the store a bill of righteous indignation will
go up

slighted and slandered and salivating
at the thought of the pain that will be inflicted
get back
get back
the courts exist for the purpose of getting back at
people
all that wrong
and you so strong
run away here comes king kong

rudely misinterpreted the scripture seemed out of
place
and all the lack of grace
the light was not shining clearly
amidst the vulgar interpretation the clowns
could not hide
wipe that smile and that smirk off thy face herr
spazwart
to the temple to buy some bread
breaking it with the peasants who live in the barracks
the glass of wine will have to wait
the finances are not in order and the teeth need
fixing and
don't even ask

waiting for the light to change
impatient and planning a great project
I thought you were coming
changed my mind
felt scared

this is not my land or my people
strangers glare at me as if
an imposter
belong to something - a religion or a club or a
business
this aimless drifting without an anchor will make you
crazy
truth is overrated
honesty is a slippery slope
take all those highminded morals - throw them in the
mud and trample them
the light turns to green and I'm homeward bound
what a relief

there's a bad moon rising
the end is predicted by fogerty
and it's more true now than ever before
the prophets are staring at the moon with glazed eyes
ed is sitting there too with his bible beside him
wondering if the lord's arrival is at hand
his 65 pontiac parrisienne is parked in three hills
waiting
the trip is coming - the midnight special and camrose
is waiting
caroline is also waiting
along with the twins and all the others
when will the lord come back
it's been some time now and it's getting crazy
even as the minds are getting hazy
and the believers are getting lazy

not doing the lords work and going to bars
and movie houses
even drinking spirits and not handing out tracts
come boys - good news - good new boys
drowning in a sea of never-ending bad news
hit over and over again
like hell forever and ever
hey Job what's for dinner
for some life is too hard and the stress leads to early
death
the single female parent after abandonment by her
mate
most men are absolute pigs
and that is why
women will eventually rule the world
and I'm okay with that
of course there are some women who are also
barbaric swine

count out the number of revelations
none
a life without a spiritual component is something
weird and unsustainable

when the future becomes the past
there were scientists who wondered and theorized
whereby could eternity be challenged
jumping into the void
avoiding the collisions as matter
turned

did you see the spirits as immortality was preserved
it was a compelling vulnerability
as waves of time
collide and sprinting forth
a new universe

a slave to sin we cannot be
or the right we lose to be free

over in New York City the cowgirls with bells on
their toes
letting themselves go
trying to lasso some form of
what's that - fashion on the loose
corral all those modern ideas
left back in time
turned on a dime
stuck in a pile of grime
bobby was in his prime

the crowd hissed and booed

throw the saddle on the old grey mare
a slow pace
not going to win the race
and there ain't no grace
cause the loser will get some mace
on their face

violent overtures of decadent rock and roll

who is over in the corner praying
is it a young dude named frank

he was an Einstein non-believer
not buying the product even though heavily endorsed
by science guys everywhere
time oh time what are you that you play with us and
spit out such a cacophony
like chickens dancing in the yard
and never looking up to see the mountains and
dream
it really makes me scream

I can't accept it
I won't accept it
well what proof have you
no real proof but a feeling inside that rejects the
public acclamation
some experiential notifications that came about with
book learning and
observation of the world around
what is the criteria for the making of sense
when do ideas rise up to acceptance
remember when everyone thought the earth was flat
accepted dogma
but we learned and changed our views - most of us
christians believe the earth is 6000 years old
add up the dates in the bible and presto - they got no
choice
a christian who believes in evolution ceases to be a

christian or
was never one in the first place
it stands up to a reasonable analysis
correct me if I am wrong professor
rebuke my logic if thou canst
black and white

all those deals made without a thought for ethics
lies and distorted half-truths
it's all driving me insane
everyone is lying about so many things and we can't
find the truth
so again we have to ask - what is the truth
subjective
how I hate that word because it throws logic into a
tailspin
now we go in circles
dizzy and confused
such a perilous journey and for most
still sitting or
sleeping
what
rubbing the eyes

and it was with a very succinct appreciation of
confusion
that
the Renaissance was understood to be a new way
and old water must be poured out upon it for
the mavericks would have it no other way

days like this
double-stress with madness and
sadness and
badness combined with
dreams in pink and green and violet that
rose up like balloons until a bad-humoured clown
pricked them with a needle

it needn't have been that way at all
lamented the old people living in the old manor by
the bay
music could have been played and tempers tempered
now only debris is collecting on the roundabout
round and round we still go and who's getting off
and whereto

to the city of bones
shuddering eyes shifting
unholy is this scene before us
and thoughts race as once full of reverence
become
scattered
I imagined the past when flesh and blood was part of
the equation and the breath
of life
now - silent
a graveyard with bleached bones
forsaken
alone

knock on wood laid back warrior
your pursuit of victims while
sitting in your undergarments
is laughable even
deplorable
and the sleeping virgins
dream
but with closed eyes the night
remains dark
so lonely
so terrifying
so sad
hands reaching out to heaven
the sick
the lame
the abused - please where and
when will it end
prostrate lying and begging
all those blessings from above
flying promises that turn
even as the stomachs churn
shine
shine the light

in the forest - the big bad wolf
all those victims of pleasure
hand in hand
hiding behind trees running
escaping
the hot city in the heels

together with the the predators - who
live in the hollow
side shuffle - jump
always a helpless falling down

somehow our characters dematerialized
transforming into hysterical vagabonds
shuffling down the back alleys of civilization
losing our marbles and
shrugging each other's shoulders
a pathetic consequence

Chapter Four

walking without wondering if the road leads
somewhere
the man said that the compass didn't work
bold strokes on the canvass
belying an inner strength
not true exclaimed the boxer
I have no money
what
no money
then - fight - or
trudge depressingly in the footsteps of all who went
before
creatures of habit not
willing
come on now a change is gonna do you good

where is my servant
where is my butler
where is my gardener

up on the high wire a balancing feat
walking across a rope
no net underneath
only the rapids 100 meters below
the rope snaps
the artist falls
and dies

when words fall on deaf ears then
the hands go up in frustration
no response
like talking to a wall
hello
anybody home
nothing
no response
rude and uncivilized n'est pa

who said the line was straight and who can confirm it
the surveyor
original organic orgasm
she wanted one and prayed for one and one day
whilst dressed in crisp white linen it happened
forget about a halo
it was no accident

freddy dreamt of owning a digging machine
move that dirt here
and then
there
a big truck to move it here
and then
there

there's yeast
in the east
but it's best
in the west

unite the politician screamed as he stole money from
the treasury
oh I'm such a sneaky guy
no one will catch me
and I can buy nice things and eat good food
oh I'm so happy
the people are so naive and stupid
I have a good life and I steal all the time
ha ha ha

the judge said you are guilty but
let's see
pay me some money and free you go
what about justice and integrity
integrity is overrated
cash is king
thank you herr judge - you are too kind

I found a lawyer once who didn't lie
ha ha just kidding
what a funny one that was
as if

innocence where have you gone
and how
is it lost
after all
a precious commodity that hustlers were selling
was it the cheap perfume
or a sold-out performance on willy's couch
frail and ageing
tears
bending in the wind
snapping
take my hand
it's yours forever and this love
let it be your defence

chains in the moonlight
silhouettes against an angry sky
the deep longing for justice
why do you disrespect civilization
people in power
wielding disproportionate control
treating us like animals
like trash
I want to smash
and mash

their heads and then crash
the ongoing party

sitting on the green green grass
Silvia eating a coffee crisp
smiling from ear to ear
spirituality realized and reaching out for that higher
ground

see see see
standing in a field of pink and yellow roses
the artistic narcissist with the black sign
transference of evil doctrine
zig zag
the wheels were integral
and interspersed between
a sense of social disconnect - just shows how
versatile and deceptive are
the riders
that cultural space where echoes of art are heard
amidst the fascist mythology
where greek gods and
independent philosophers conspire
it's a showdown after all
sarcastic little nitwit
preaching a political satire whilst standing on
protocol

the defection was seen as a blow to the ruling party
would there be more traitors

the cause was being challenged
serious repercussions could result
a future in jeapardy
the people were restless and shifting
on one leg and then on another
finding a comfortable position is hard sometimes
especially in a windstorm
changes and opinions
moods reflecting a weakening of resolve or perhaps
fear

when the planets are aligning
there is talk of the rock star resigning
with all the pretty ladies reclining
and the soldiers declining
to fire their weapons at the revolutionaries

they went to the garden to pray
they vowed to stay
all day
and ask god to make the murderous rulers pay
for the atrocities they committed down by the bay

when will we have justice
respect is hiding in the tall grass beating it's chest
in the secret room the rich plan for greater profits as
the children of the poor suffer
neglect and poverty collide in a sorrowful crash
will we never gather enough willpower and defeat
these evil forces among us

screaming and shouting and shooting
forward march

when we are down we always turn
to god
in god we trust
even as we lust
and long to lie in beds of lace and silk
abba father forgive us and give
us back some measure of power so
we can assert ourselves and become real
men and women lacking
for nothing
becoming free to speak our minds

can a tube of paint be your weapon of choice
formidable fashionable frustrations
sneaking up on you like a wolf
are you lost - in that superdark forest and then
falling
in the ditch the brainwashed robbers wait
torture me not oh princes of darkness
pierce me not with scissors that are symbolic of great
power
against the legs
the red paint splashing
martyrs intent on developing good feelings and
projecting a stimulating essense
a therapeutic activity with angry overtones
take that crayon and smear it on the concrete wall

well - get on the stage then and
sing
dance
I see your mask and you're not fooling anyone
mad dictators are running away into the theatre
it's out of order says the nun as she lifts up her skirt
the pounding of the fist on the mural in front of the
bank
we need our insanity and
can the reminder be authentic
then pay your fines and eat your doughnuts

I opened up all the doors
and behold- the crystal ship sailing to distant shores
she said - how absurd
and the butler answered - yes and extravagant and
impressive
at which time the maid interjected - so what
it was all true in an ironic and pretentious way
peter peter which way then
off to America and may England rot
as the stench of her royals encompasses the land
let the overture commence then and may all that
vanity be damned
such a circus - moaned the rock and roll queen

architecturally speaking the design was a
contradiction
voices were out of sync
is everyone expressing themselves

or only the rich the rude and the vulgar
what about the meek and shy and poor
screwed over again and again
no say
no status
no respect
this world is pregnant with injustice
a sign on every corner
help me and
what about me and
hear me
order among all this disorder
the chaos is choking us
like smog
the oxygen of orderliness we need
dark at the bottom with black in the centre lower
plane
then yellow and light in upper right
with some light blue and white smeared hither and
yon
the painter paints in the corner of the church
he is not happy
in a deep funk
but he carries on and finally he throws his paintbrush
against the wall
done and he's not happy
he's never happy
c'est la vie

igor took a big swig of freedom and choked

as he stumbled down the stairs of tolerance he
clutched his throat
he finally fell down upon his face in a pool of
anything goes and
was stabbed to death by a refugee from Syria
poor poor refugee was not to blame the media
chanted
he had been traumatized and so had the right to kill
igor
what about igor
well, you know, it's like...whatever
after the great struggle the children were sad poor
and distraught so
the great mother from across the waters held them in
her arms and coddled them
she breastfed them and protected them
the babies grew but expected the mother to protect
them forevermore
the mother finally said forget about it
now the children who are adults are crying and
carrying on
bad mother they scream
how dare you abandon us
grow up she admonishes
still they cry bitterly
she shrugs her shoulders

your ideology is not sitting well with me
where are values that can enhance the human
experience for

everyone
not just the bloody rich
or connected
or royalty
or beautiful people
or selfish
or rude
take your value-less ideology which is most likely
based on a religion
and stuff it

i'm rocking on my porch
in my hand is a torch
and I'm going to torch
your pretentious diabolical symbols of power
we will not bow to you
we will not kiss your asses
we will not be your slaves
true freedom is based on real and lasting equality
for everyone
this is a shared existence
hello

the american dream is a sham
come here and work hard and make others your slaves
so you can
spoil yourself like a king while others wait on you
and sleep under bridges
and their children have no healthcare and they cry
their teeth hurt and they beg for food

how dare you
you fat and pompous obnoxious anti-human animals
living in your penthouse and fancy digs and going to
your fancy clubs
may you burn in hell - a hell we will make for you
you thieves who strip us of our humanity
we hate you rich people because you are killing us
and our hands are tied
please someone untie us and set us free
and we will kill the oppressors - these terrorists who
torture our children
and take our land and our substance and our pride
unrighteousness must end
because we will not bend
as you offend
and send
us to early graves

it's time to be free
and you will see
that we
will happy be

we lie in pain
our futures going down the drain
as our strengths wane
and the rich beat us with a cane
but we will take off the chain
and then it will come - the rain

superseding basic humanness was a concept of god
subconscious mental activity transformed him
into a giant father with a long white beard
his book however was more or less expressionism
the interpretations left up to the readers or listeners
sometimes very zen
and sometimes very fascist

names were called
roll calls revisited
this game
where spectators were left
speechless

ghostly images projected on ancient ruins
a heartfelt issuance
yet
none will be left standing as the kingdom rises to
heaven
and then

musicians appearing on clouds
magic
the desire faded as the years
old faded ripped up jeans
fashion
and then
ziggy appeared with his own leper messiah
and the masses gasped
sacrilege barely tolerated but the road was paved for

superstar
horrified and shocked we threw in the towel
as even the writings of Lewis couldn't console us
and perelandra slunk into the shadows
as dylan flirted with salvation
a castrated jewish mind thrown into chaos

can crazy warnings save the prophet
the happiness
vanishing
the mist a simple referendum
enlightened mysticism
the gods will surely strike
as wheels go
round and
round

take the hand of the rejected lover
he prays to the figures in his garden
imploring
love was random
arrows missing the mark

the ufo was identified
names attached
sobriety guaranteed
why are all the promises broken

hopeless the lovers cry
waiting and eating hotdogs

who died to save your soul
who played you that rock and roll
who scored the winning goal
who sat upon the skinny pole

all those plastic moments were so
well
searching for peace
still
the guitar combines with the violin as the preacher
reads
revelation and
the dancer moves silently on the dance floor
as blades of truth rise up through the floorboards

the constipated rocker threw the ball through the
broken window
stand up
giddy with joy they vanished and then
jets flying to the promised land
the pilot wearing a jesus hat
and far away the angels
blowing on trumpets
even as the lone hipster dufus was educating himself
in a bathroom stall

music rings in our ear
and that lonely tear
a jerker really
heaven help us in this desolate land

scavengers we are
scurrying like rats

run johnny run
don't stop to smell the roses
don't trip
it's a perilous journey that you're on
why oh why
why do the demons chase you
will you outrun them or
hide somewhere
I don't envy you johnny
poor poor guy

knocking on heavens door is not for the feeble-
minded
knock knock
anyone there
jesus
god
moses

dylan must know and if he doesn't he can always ask
zimmerman
if music must befriend your inner alter ego
then
happy to accommodate

who's doing all the talking
in circles

bereft of undone tasks that
tease and castigate
all at once
before and after
while Alice runs to the mountains and cuts off her
hair

who wrote that number on the cheesecloth
as the water seeped mysteriously
forward march and goosestepping
be careful of the ducks who are crossing the road

the letter incited violent overtures
the guns and wars and bayonets
competing for the glory
of lords and demons and generals
disfigured
mutilated
embarrassed
cut the ties and shoot to kill
the blood
she died on calvary
the remission for our sins

now naked and exposed she scratches in the gutter
saliva dripping
open wounds bleeding
oh god I was wondering
please I know the deserving end of the scale was left
in the rain

rusty
borrow me ten years of remission

streetwise and ignorant
give me that
kick it here
who
despite the objections I still fell asleep on the couch
and then there were all those government workers
sneaking into the banquet hall

I like cotton candy
rotten teeth as a consequence
peace with a side of burned fries
crunchy and munchy
running around the barn eating chow mein

they evacuated the ditch
why are they there
laughing at the memory
bullets
changing jobs in the middle of the night
trading
as parading all those headless bodies

one two
three
four
baking cookies inside the nuclear reactor
a five-count instituted as a protocol for a baked

overdose
lounging on those sidewalks with
see and come - wait
minutes and
a new king crowned and fooled
somewhat

when the rage is pulling us in another direction
grab a basket of ancient artifacts
meet me at the corner
where he met she and she was blonde
and for tomorrow why not brown
a tone here or there
matters it and will we still eat porridge at sunset

a lifeline then
overthrown but on standby
the blackboard beckoned and reproached
me a sinner and thou -
well I heard that a graceless fool would suffice
the task as not becoming or demanding
and the martians were casting the deciding vote
it was an understanding but was it something
or nothing
or not at all
then there was all that preaching and pontificating
a hoax perhaps
enamoured
clamoured
sedated

please my dear pass the schnapps
and
love is still rated
as even all were hated
and berated
we shouted and screamed for mercy
faded souls tarnished with
blemishes exposed and
coated with insinuations
corrected and indirectly disposed

blue blue betrayal
come with me all ye
the sacrilege of abundance is shown
Alice laughing at all the horror
even as she cowers so sad in the corner
still marching steadily onwards
as dazed and mortified the silver state trooper
staggered on
the boogeyman is here
drinking scottish beer
oh let us all be glad
no time to get all sad

the return of the wise men to the stable
bringing decorum to the table as the bells were
ringing
using many tools
to shut down all the fools
pull out the knife

shut down the strife
laugh in the faces
of all the basket cases
making a case for the sensible
kicking out the reprehensible
ànd the dirty uncouth
then lighting the tree of truth

hear ye hear ye
ye shall be free
of slander bigotry and hate
as we wipe clean the slate

rejoice oh nations of this earth
of merriment and joy there shall be no dearth
showers of blessing we shall feel
and all the temple bells will peal

the king is riding through the gates
even as the devil still masterbates
the sword is sharp that he shall wield
and the naked demon he shall yield

the king will cut the imposter to shreds
and cut off all his henchmen's heads
all evil he will eradicate
the party boys will meet their fate

then shall the righteous dance for joy
and they shall say - oh boy oh boy

tis good to have a mighty king
and have a brand new song to sing

hosanna in the highest will be the cry
as we all sit down to pumpkin pie
we'll drink our beer and cucumber gin
and throw our winnings in the bin

no more nightmares - only dreams
eating many krispy creams
no more nightmares no more fright
only faces filled with delight

Chapter Five

emotions cloud our perception
or inform us
lost
forlorn with no grasp of truth
what you doin man
thought you were a fighter

we see
but only
what we want to
knock knock knock
trapped inside a box
snapping our fingers to imaginary subordinates
da da da

the lead guitar is riffing
the dog is sniffing
but there isn't a window

here - take this saw and cut a hole

we are reluctant to cut a hole in a box
please
a bagel with lox
a cappaccino

the light
surreal but swinging in the wind
casting it's rays
upon a scene
yesterday scavenging at the seashore
with seasick seagulls suffocating

up the beach a conductor
wearing a cap backwards as if
the baton making figure 8's in the air
as the dancers gathered shells
with a choir of virgins singing on the rocks
and wearing white socks
oh no
ho ho ho
lift up your voices
and hello
to you and you and you
the saxophones step up

wailing
then walked Jesus Christ
barefoot
his tears falling in sorrow for this sinful generation
arms outstretched
why god why

sensitivity in the dark forest
a truce
then who will experience the fires of hell
and the biting from the goblins

all the animals are not going to become vegetarians
overnight
we need time for evolution to work
mr. lion from now on thou shalt eat only grass
grass my ass

listen the train is blowing its horn
taking a trip
far away
another lord is calling
so please step up
stop stalling
pack up your suitcase
leave your security behind
venture out

an sos
the heart is fragile

so please
don't go
but the mountains are calling
and heaven too
it's a competition

why lay down and die
try
sit up
look at the sky
so blue
and the birds - soaring - gliding
life

there he sits
the pianist playing
filling the air with incidentals and
fragments of harmonies and bits of
melody
almost incoherent and still
connected
life is - a journey and is not always
smooth
a bumpy ride
and then sometimes - a transcendence
or a replacement
a life is a shining star
burning brightly
in a furnace of desire and hope
we grope

feeling our way along the floor
looking for a door
to escape
crying
begging
screaming
for freedom
even as we wonder what is free

how much baggage do you have
your ticket
this way please
don't bump your head

in the country
free
imagine if it isn't true
a desert
obscure illusions are pressing upon your fantasies
reality is only a heartbeat away

bangles dangle from her ear
they jangle as she dances
she doesn't have a hat on
she drinks labatts blue
and dances alone
at the club
as the band plays
and sings songs of deliverance

the old man sat at the counter of the diner
eating chicken noodle soup
he looked poor
ripped up pants
unkempt beard and long straggly hair
I looked into his eyes and saw
a reflection
not of a bank building but
of myself
a stab of pain
my destiny

the streetlight shines
creating shades
inside this circle of illumination
we find a questionable consideration
as we wonder
inside ourselves who are we
a creation
a creator
who

a man in a brown suit jacket steps onto the street
he exits the light
a backwards glance
a wistful look

we cover ourselves with blankets
precious symbols
metaphors of love

created by our mothers
their love sewn inside
mama

the lead guitar stretches out the high notes
wailing
and the singer with arms flailing
whispers
memories of our perceptions of Jesus across a screen
flashes
the symbol crashes
the lights go out
the people go home
crawl into their beds
under their blankets
and sigh
some cry
some dream
goodnight

sweet sweet Jane
why are you so insane
jumping from port to port
and singing lusty songs about love
confuscious say woman in love is
dangerous
beware of her stilletos
they serve a double purpose

words die

when lovers lie
held hostage
as ransoms are demanded
they cannot flee
even as they see
that they are trapped

down by the sea
the pigs did squeal
as they ate their feed
chop and potato peels
then they flew away
like geese
this was told to me by a lawyer
who appeared to be quite normal
so I had no reason to doubt him
if a musician had told me this tale
well I would have had cause for doubt
it's not that I generalize
or discriminate
or put people into boxes
not at all
even if tales are tall
but I must confess that I never knew
that pigs could fly
you learn something new every day

the mothership
ready to sail
space travel is scary

even as the immigrant women were hairy
with unshaved armpits and legs
fresh off the boats
discounting a new reality and misunderstanding
the protocols

did Jesus drink whisky before he was crucified
and did he write the New Testament
before Paul saw the light
wild days
in the judean wilderness with the devil
taking trips to church steeples
and clashing with the ideology of the Romans
and allowing the high priest his moment

as he was dying the disciples were playing pool
the barmaid looks at peter
you were his friend
no
never
not I
thought I saw you in the news
whatever
another beer
ya

judas took the red eye to New York
he had a date with John and Yoko
to write new music
hey there judas you got any dough

ya man - thirty pieces of silver

it's a heartless world
so please go take a walk
watch the whales off the coast
blowing water into the air
feeling the sea air on your face
a peaceful feeling
this oasis in a troubled world

what are we going through
who can understand
how can we defend
our answers
when
there are only questions
and
the sensors have taped our mouths shut
we scream
but not a sound
only a muffled hum

it's a noiseless world
as the boom of anguish is stiffled
we fear truth
we're scared of admitting it
insecure
frantic
frightened
we protest in vain

no one is listening

a vision of a starry starry night
blinds us
dear Vincent what did you know
what were you trying to say
lying under the streetlight
in the gutter of the street
as the dealers deal
the cops arrest them
later they are released and the trade continues
catch and release
it's a government program

where is the sky
is my altimeter correct

the music softly plays
sitting on the sofa
meditating with a cook book
cnn on the tv
another war
another murder
another drowned migrant

going to the movies was never going to be an option
to replace a good book
but things change
boredom evolves
into depression

and excitement is the antidote
therefore a movie with popcorn was in order
and a side effect - becoming socialized

in terms of being sad
a look at personal circumstances
what role does a shrink play
as little as possible
find a play to go to
go to a concert
start painting

sleeping is of course a wonderful past time
a good bed is a requisite
good pillows a must - exquisite down
colourful comforters and blankets
even some teddy bears
cosytown

she slipped into her big bathtub
a bubble bath
sweet and thoughtful scents
candles expressing a comforting warmth
music playing
a return to God

why are doctors such egocentric psychopaths
domineering
arrogant
without any bedside manners

as if raised by bears
devoid of the human touch
and we depend on them to heal us
it's a contradiction
terrorists who make us afraid
fearful amid an horrific dependency
and as they experiment many are killed
it's a crap shoot
hope to be one of the lucky ones
as they cram
medicine
down our throats and
inject serum into our veins
there you go mortal
take it and go

go where

cover me with kindness and consideration
shower me with gifts of frankincense and myhr
and adore all that my spirit is
the wretched and the weak
they wait
while the great suppress their desire to monopolize
instead they tranquilize the masses
with drugs
and then rape them
belittle them
disrespect them
and open doors to the outer systems

there where opportunity is banned
and repetition without meaning is encouraged

into the pot
this and that
stirred up and served
on a bed of inclusive bitterness

and so it was that the city council met underneath a
street lamp
in the evening to discuss the latest crime wave
standing in the gathering darkness they
covered their faces with their hands
and moaned
and groaned
woe is us what can we do
we are attacked on every side
and our hands are tied
the criminals have so many rights that we cannot
stop them anymore
we are bound up in knots
justice has been chased away by the kindness freaks
and forgiveness has become the morning star

alone in a canoe on a northern lake
watching the moon go marching across the sky
with the northern lights
dancing
dreaming of a fire
with flames shooting out

and spitting

down south the Kentucky derby was being held
flowers for the winner

slashing and burning
murmuring and stammering
everyone has their manna moment
had enough

the red lipstick schmear on the mirror was a stylish
overture
an invitation to steal second base
the coach waving you in
and a white rapper pulling down her pants
and flashing
the peace sign

clap for the wolfman
okay
guess who exhorted us to do that
and who broke up with their american woman
it wasn't king tut
what

if you climb upon the watchtower
will you see
five hundred lepers
running after you
heal me oh son of david

or tom
or levi
the helicopter arrives from the hotel California

inside the seminary all the priests were practising
masterbation
technique is everything
so as to prevent a premature ejaculation
and salvation

I can hear them say
welcome to the ranch
get on your horse and ride
first one to the fence is the winner
what do we win mr.ranch
you win the right to speak your mind

the lady is singing on the stage of the penthouse
and she doesn't have on one shred of clothing
naked
the band is on fire
the drummer is throwing his sticks into the audience

pack up all your stuff
enough
off to Mars to have a vacation
don't forget your antigravity lotion
or your pretzels
crunch crunch

I saw a violent person punch a wall
and then discretely walk away
such a diabolical disorder

on the corner the preacher was preaching from a
book
the communist manifesto by Karl
do all things together
get rid of profit
make all things equal
such wonderful thoughts
do away with riches and the rich
the audience applauded
freedom they shouted
love reigns
Jesus is lord

the band plays at the bandstand
as the dog pees on the stand
oh pardon me dearest conductor master
speaking of fun
narcissism is a favourite pastime
and goes well with popcorn and a bottle of gin

flying
when you're dying
what a fantastic liberation
see you cruel and heartless world
the laughter taunts
clowns in the trees

pointing at the annoying humans
where is the gun when you need one
let's buy some bullets at the supermarket
and get some magazines

the final resting place of unadulterated magic
abra ca da bra
under the rigging and cloaked in a fanciful array of
munitions
a confederate hold out
it was a partnership with creatures who in fetal
positions
postulated that the law of averages was
erased a long time ago and supplanted by
the charismatic arts council of Nicea
where street art supplanted the law of the jungle
see it this way
don't prepare for succession either
because no king will tolerate it
and so the artist completed his painting at the
skatepark
even as the superintendent of the local chapter of
chalkpainting
fell down some stairs at the university

those narrow dark corridors of learning
turned loose and wondering about
the various theories
and then given an award for being a success at
factory art

come on people watch the show at the culture
consortium
those surreal transformative intricate drawings
created a visual contradiction because
there was a dichotomy that wasn't evident until
one stood at the vortex of the coordinates
there where the architectural features faded into the
surrounding culture
similarly a pop up was installed at the sewage plant
raw sewage mixed with oil paints and smeared
upon the rafters

the guests were outraged and
electrified
a reaction totally inspired by the avantegarde
custodians
who not knowing what to do
reached into their bag of tricks
and sold torn kickers in the hall

still it was all so serene and quiet as if
nothing out of the ordinary had taken place but
it was known that the curator was having an affair
with the chef de cuisine
a powerful analogy which pointed to otherworldly
connections
where space Cowboys were trying to break in
patching electricity to their body parts
and detonating various powder kegs of frustration
a gruelling battle

a dedicated rigging of emotions

flooded with complaints there was no choice
the roof had to be replaced
and the columns refurbished
with roads barricaded off to accommodate the
construction
even as Anita sizzled in a one piece
and the dean apologized for acting so demure

Chapter Six

there was a communication breakdown
over a cup of coffee and a croissant
5 packets of sugar and
two teaspoons of cream
taste
so subjective
very important to the individual

the outlaws rode into the sunset
bags of money in their saddlebags
with them rode a couple of fishermen from Gallilee
Andrew and Simon
they spoke in parables about a great teacher
who taught them on his iPad
he was a sorcerer who conjured up wine at weddings

and
healed the sick and raised the dead
and spoke about a coming great kingdom
in the end he was executed by the Italians
who made shoes out of his skin

as they rode eagles soared overhead
in their beaks palm branches and on the feet
sandles
they came to a pass where some soldiers stood guard
what's the password they shouted out
saving grace was the reply
right on brothers
come on through
and so they rode thru the pass and into the vast
plains beyond

behind the outlaws some distance away rode a posse
of Pharasees
their badges glinting in the sun
guns at their sides ready
to shoot the outlaws dead
they came to the pass
what's the password the soldiers bellowed
we don't know it
what
and so they shot them all dead
and the eagles backtracked and ate their carcasses
blessed be the name of the lord the soldiers shouted
in him is all power and might

forever and ever and ever
amen

then the soldiers lifted their hands to heaven
and lo the lightening struck across the sky
and the thunder crashed
then it rained for 40 days and 40 nights
after that a rainbow appeared and
a dove alighted on the shoulder of the soldiers
it is well with our souls they sang
as the sun shone brightly on the plains

will you be a servant
will you wash the feet of the bums
will you clothe them in satin and rubies
all power is given unto you
so saith the lord god Jahovah

and he will wash away your sins
you will be white as snow and
clean as a mountain stream
untarnished

watch the politicians as they lie
corrupted by this world
seduced by the promise of power
lying in beds of compromise
with shady accomplises
jealousy
conceit

greed
deception
they torture us with broken promises
and beat us in the shadow of the garden

the distorted reality
which a cracked mirror
enhances
the essense of classical despair
shut the windows
draw the curtains
turn on the music
burn some incense
paint something on a canvass
good thoughts be banished
allow the monsters to roam freely and sulk

the sinner dreamed not of heavens choirs but
of roaring and shining cars
of sex with beautiful maidens
airplanes that soar
and a loaded revolver pointed at his head
sending him to another galaxy
where walking on narrow ledges was a favourite
pastime
past the window as a witch opens it up and
shrieks loudly
don't look up
she throws cliches into the faces

over in Russia the strong man said - we need more weapons
so we can be stronger than the west
let's have a party and drink wine and eat Big Macs
and apple pie
with ice cream cones
pizza too
invite the Italians
let the dancing begin and pass the peanut butter
where's the jam mister
grab your crown pister
and shoot the pirates who are trying to bust in
it's a heartless world and
drown your sorrows
we need more weapons of mass destruction
more atomic bombs to obliterate our enemies

stop the invaders who are raping our women
killing our children
they kill them in the womb
help us oh god
save us from this barbarianism
they stalk us and write our names on the walls of
their temples
in the caves up high the monks live and pray to God
for our salvation
they read the bible and eat rice and beans
ringing bells and watching World War Two movies
heil hitler and pass the tablets of acid
we need to be transformed

a transfiguration is in order
and all the misfits we will shelter
come to us all ye
who are weak and heavy laden
and you will find rest in our caves
and please
disregard the bats

let them eat cheeseburgers and pancakes with honey
breaking bread with all the druggies is the will of
God
who loves the broken-hearted and heals their spirit
but the sporty rich bastards in their spandex panties
he will destroy
sending their souls down to Sheol
where the demons will eat their essence and spit
them out into hell
there they will be tried and tortured
endless pain and misery
their due for living high on the hog and not sharing
the city lights
and the feeling of loneliness and despair
how to survive and get along with all the racists
voices were calling my name
as pictures of my pants on fire were flashing on the
billboard
and then Warhol descended from heaven on a cable
constructed of toilet paper
living in a metaphor
it's an illusion that lives with this circle spinning out

of control
it's as hard as it seems
and to the left a scarecrow
the crows are flying away
caw caw

peter riding his bicycle round and round
his heart is bleeding on his sleeves
his sins have been exposed
damned by God to live with the riders of the storm
in L.A.
there by the black cat crosswalk where the killers walk
and the lesbians talk with
strangers who play with their zippers
scowling sarcastically and
sneering
are those loonies standing beside the boat
or girls that are taking their men by the hand
and loving them

Einstein is standing in front of of the garbage bin
with Darwin lying inside
covered up with the garbage both of them have
written
God is overhead sending down thunderbolts with
Obama
howling in a helicopter that hovers overhead

who will be worthy to be granted an interview
with his royal highness the pope of England

are you unique enough
what is your expertise and claim
to fame
exhausted the frowners fall down on the floor
as she looks on with a scowl on her face

take up residency in Harlem
it's a neighbourhood for the poor in spirit
people that Jesus likes and blesses
they anticipate racism and heartache and depair
every home is curated
no fathers allowed here
a bevy of infamous orgies
an accompaniment to squaller
oh ya baby lets settle down here
a good place to rear the kids with many bullet
infested fields

a screwed up version of femininity
that is rebuked by the men it is rebelling against
with the protagonist begging for a crumb
of respect
even as she kicks him when he's down
it's a desperate conversion to accepting a poetic
interpretation of
a woman's right to disrespect herself
down on her knees
blowing the world as she farts
leaving traces of her sins in the gutter of relevance

get on your knees and pray
sinners in heaven and on earth
everyone is feeling bad
except the righteous religious rappers
who read the bible as it lies upon a naked ass
blessed be the new constitution
get ready for a new revolution
as we fool everyone into thinking that we care
magical conversations in darkened corners of our
sanctimonious minds
that reek of fish and eggs
and narcistic inspiration

look at the weirdos
watch them run to the cliff
and jump off into the sea
and drown

a heap of trouble mr.schnabel
under the street lamp I stand again
shadows are gathering
like storm clouds
and what can I see
only what you want me to see
blankets are hung up on the clothesline
of the Vatican
I used to hide in a room with the pope
whispering
plotting
second guessing

then crawling around in some pipes
looking for a reward
so forgiveness could take place and not only for me
but for all of mankind
they encircle me to destroy me
treat me like I'm nothing
ignore me and exclude me from their conversations
till I move away and sit by myself
it always ends that way
I am nothing
worthless
not worthy of human interaction
I have nothing to say
I am space
disrespected and ignored
my meaningless existence is sad and debilitating
I stumble in the darkness of my existence
as people try to avoid me
going to the other side of the street
I speak but no one listens
I am not interesting
I have no experiences
I have no property or money or fame or stature
and so I sink into nothingness
they bully me with their arrogance
and so silence has become me

don't roll the dice
instead sing the blues
and eat some watermelon salad with sockeye salmon

under the lights the mermaids swim and bat their
eyelashes

at the end of the lane turn right and you will find a
pile of treasure
hiding under a green Volkswagen bus
open the passenger door
count to 10
say doopy poopy pie and wink three times
then the bus will rise two feet and move forward 10
feet
exposing the treasure in a hole
there are 50 bars of gold there
enjoy

sometimes good things are hiding right in front of
you
and all you need to know is the code
and then you can access all that treasure
keep your eyes open
and your ears too

the bible is without end
it is eternal
deeper than the deepest deep
unfathomable
in it we can lose ourselves forever and never
exhaust it's wisdom
try to understand what it says
or means

try to find a way to see who and what is God
if confuses as it teaches
and bewilders those who try to usurp it

in a vision I found myself in a semi-desert landscape
there were cacti and old weathered buildings
off in the distance I saw what looked like a sculpture
it was two columns of concrete about 4 feet square
towering into the air 40 feet high
across the columns spanned a large wooden beam
and from this beam hung a multitude of guitars
there were Taylors and Gibsons and Martins
I even spotted a violin

they gather at the museum and stare into the eyes
of the sketches of human misery
painted there by a fake Picasso
who knowing something he thought no once else
knew
entertained artistic notions of special despair
painting his interpretations on the walls
hallucinating from bouts of irreverence
where he subjected the tenets of Christianity to
a mocking sarcasm
where is your messiah he begged

the keys to heaven indeed
and pray tell where is this heaven

take a sprig of juniper and mix

it
with ten hail Marys
a little frankincense
and myhr
throw in a bit of angels we have heard on high
and sweetly
sing a song of sixpence
as you cartwheel
down
the place Ravignan
and rummage around in the Bateau-Lavoir looking
for
fundamentals of fashion

I saw an angel fly in space
she had a sparkly face
all decked out in sentiments of grace
and pinkish hues of lace

Chapter Seven

she screwed up her face as she drank the sour drink
sweetness was lacking
flavour is the spice
and it's nice
to have a bit of fashion to go with
heartache

Picasso and Fernande
together they set the stage for future fashion
sensibility
she the muse
he the facilitator of her style
out of pain
she changed the game and set
the world

on a new course and made picasso great

it was so fine
when he moved the stein
and made her see
that he
was a force to be reckoned with
as together with braque
whose intuition he did lack
he changed the world

so when you paint your pictures
and play the clavier
think on these things and remember
you are not alone
for others too are searching for their pot of gold
among the colours that come together
and play among each other on canvases
on paper
and on walls everywhere

art is the great deceiver
promising so much even as it tricks the appraiser
into
thinking that there is much more to discover
than there really is
and yet
it mystifies and defies
logic
speaking in nuances that seduce

and cajole

what was the intent
from whence did this spring from
who is it representing
where is it going

on and on the questions rage
as without answers the painting hangs
staring into the space that separates itself
from the banality of life
regal and arrogant
strong and weak
vulnerable and pleading
for relevance

walking through London with the memory of
Kossoff
how different it all feels now
like I'm knocking on heavens door
in the doorway of the cathedral - Larry Norman
his long blonde hair blowing in the wind
a version of Warhol

will you be ready when God begins the apocalypse
Angels will be blowing trumpets
water will turn red
Egypt's plagues revisited
Jesus will establish gods kingdom on earth
Jerusalem will be destroyed and a new one built

the devil will be thrown into the pit
and the armies will gather for Armageddon
gonna be real cool
just like the movies
who's going to play Jesus
maybe a black woman
even bond is going that way
equal opportunity you know
don't want anyone to feel left out
or how about a Buddhist Monk

I shivered when I walked out onto the plains of
Abraham
and remembered the history
it's where the French lost a country
but gained a foothold
style over substance
nuance over flavor
except of course for the croissant
a pastry that defines the mannerisms
is it hip
who knows
who cares
find the love in shadows that gather in Paris
Picasso had to go to there to find his art
it was hanging there in the souls of the poor and
needy
and he was given the key to unlock the hearts
and expose the mysteries
divine intervention

a sinner chosen to reveal God to humanity
torn between duty and lust
enraptured by his own sexual appetite
misled by his perverted fantasies
that found a place
upon his canvasses
even as his women suffered for his indulgences
a man who disrespected and abused
reveling in his own importance
and yet
doing the will of God
a compromise and a tribute to hypocricy
playing the part of the mad lover
dissecting and demeaning so many women
in his pathetic quest for greatness
and sacrificing integrity and honesty
preferring to fornicate and test the patience of God
himself

the word was made flesh and dwelt among us
it pressed its luck until
nailed to the cross it died
and as it died it was reborn
and rose to heaven from whence it came
where it beseeches the father on our behalf
so we can all be heroes
forever and ever
just like Bowie sang
kings and queens
forever and ever

the shadows
and under the stairs
the boxer
making those fast and furious moves
a right
a left
beware
even a statue will blink
where is the pot
hiding and wary
because
memories are not long
everyone is hitting out
as lying on their beds
heads under pillows
waiting and
counting the days

the delivery is coming
and then the studying can commence
as a new career is beginning
after the inspiration
and the beauty has descended
oh sister where is your mercy
is it a slave that she is good for
a Jezebel
incarcerated
oh magdeline
please help
this laundry is a killer

the voice is drifting over the hills
like a mitchell on a mountain
the aching beauty of this servitude

where are your things
do you have nothing
even communal underwear
all the doors are shut at night
preventing the escape

the fence is a mockery to my spirit
and the weeping is keeping everyone up at night

reap what we don't sow
how will we know
as we gaze out our windows and
the gulls fly bye

the flowers
blowing and hanging around necks
the perfume so radical
woodstock
when love was
an ethereal component of inner consciousness
and everything for a little time
was easy

into the pit it all went
as the wars raged
Vietnam was a judgement from somewhere

it was the beginning and the end
as philosophers got busy
sorting it all out and waxing eloquent
but we were running on empty
awareness crept in
destroying the vibe
survive
the billboards grabbed us by the balls
squeezing
as we sang new songs of
deliverance and
rapture
as the priests call for more Hail Mary's
and the rockers for more penance

we wandered like sailers in a desert
looking for our own one night stands
gratification was hard to come by
the internet made sure everyone was informed
and we began to lose our innocence
played by the terrorists and racist accusers
as the team became defensively oriented
after all defence wins championships
who cares if we lose our humanity in the process
it all comes around again

and the dreaming was all about the garden
a longing for the peace
as Larry Normans voice cut through the fog
I am a servant

in the land of paradise she walked
in a pink bikini
beside the mountain
eating a bag of chips
and whistling a heavenly tune

beside the still waters sat the old witch
practising her spells in her mind
and wondering upon whom she would cast them
as her gaze rose to
the cloud
upon which
the dancers sit and watch
the earth convulse
and give birth to theoretical creations
as gently and solemnly
a magician transposes reality
transforming feelings
sending visions to the spiritual elite

over in the forest
the leprechauns are wearing headbands
dancing over the moss and holding twigs
waving them majestically
and casting their spells upon the creatures
it's all so blue
and who
are you

Chapter Eight

where did you come from
look inside
and what do you hope to find
a road to riches
a pathway to great wisdom
an alley to joy

chances are that you will find nothing at all
negativity can also be a blessing
and a silver lining could
balance the sheets

call it a choice
call it chance
call it a conspiracy

round and round in the cul de sac of our minds
we go
drinking gin
out of a tin
and watching the neighbours with their binoculars
as if
we were spies

they came bearing gifts
all down the street the procession moved
slowly it all emptied into the local church
it was serene
everyone was happy
and who got the gifts
they gave them to the priest
a yearly act to thank him for his blessings
he prayed to God on their behalf
and abused their children
and smiled through the tears of his remorse
they forgave him
and hoped the next year would be better
he promised again
in their hearts they knew he would fail
and so it went
year by year
tear by tear
fear by fear

pulsating current flowing
the children experiencing gestappo moments

with nobody to refresh
the memories
exhaulted historical moments
gone
transferred into an undulating subconscious
psychosis

they're lining up at the library of the black coffee
autobiographies tucked under their arms
wiping away imaginary tears
their threadbare minds polluted with humiliating
fantasies
a destructive malaise
with bullshit storms of self-indulgence exploding
as they slowly drift off into a vague nothingness
confused bitter anxious

secrets have a way of exposing themselves
laughing in their private rooms
windows open
the hood people listening outside
drinking their strong black coffee
and hoping
for eureka moments

in the beginning there was no such thing as pork fat
there was no such thing as a fat cat
nor was there a rat
or a bat

what there absolutely wasn't was reality
nothing was anything or real
abstract fantasies
complicated schemes
and theoretical possibilities

ideas were not circulating around
asking silly questions about wine and bread
they were not haphazard and incomplete
where were the germs of thought
or the non-existent entities
not even existing in someone's unexplained and
irrational mind

and so we had these hollow creations
without a creator
empty of emotion
without a biological machine
something to give birth to a spark

there are no conflicting opinions
no yin
no yang
no big Sam tang
without a thinker
or a stinker
what could be proposed
and who would it be proposed to
for without a receptor
there is no receiving

only a mish-mash of non-ideas spinning about

there was no matter
and for that matter
there was no anti-matter
even though you'd think someone would natter
on and on about such an important matter

the truth is that there cannot be truth without lies
and since there were no courts to certify a lie
and no bibles on which to swear
lies could not exist

it was a real mess
and that's why the bible says
in the beginning the world was without form and
void
devoid of meaning
exclusively non-existent

someone whispered into the apparatus
actually very loudly
from a secluded spot
behind a giant thirty-foot high hedge
they said
before anything else came along there was gravity

we say - in the beginning
but there is no beginning
there are changes

and before nothing changed there was a changeless
landscape
where the status of unintentional creation was
deliberated by no one
leaving no one breathless or
dreaming of possibilities

the philosophers did rant and rave
Nietzsche and Kant
theorizing and babbling on incoherently
about what
nothing
there wasn't anything to talk about
all conjecture and hypothesis
and lunacy
what's going on
what happened
what will happen
prophesize
we don't know
even as we can't give it a go
in the rain or on the snow
or perhaps in Kokomo
singing songs and dancing
even prancing

you may think you're reading something right now
no you're not
there is nothing on this page
double negatives be damned

cause you don't exist
not even in your own mind

if we were to suggest that there had been a lot of
stuff around forever
then we would have to ask - where did it come from
and if we named a place
the same question would have to be asked again
where did all the stuff come from
and it would become an eternal question
on and on forever without an answer
like going in circles
like the earth around the sun
elliptical but still circular

there is no end to a circular path
jump in wherever
the end is always the beginning
the alpha and the omega
smearing suntan oil on each other

all those excuses used to justify awkward alliances
all that dancing around moral goalposts
all that sleeping with enemies
for what

all the theoretical fantasies proposed by the quantum
mechanical philosophers
lead to one conclusion - neither they nor us exist

memories plunder certainty as if they have a history
trying to prove a prior existence
attempting to move the needle
from discomfort to the easychair

just because one can put their feet up doesn't mean
anything
the slaves are still working hard
the beat goes on
nothing stops trying to prove its existence
albeit hopelessly
look at me
touch me
feel me
grab the pinball machine and shake it
manipulate the balls to go into the holes
as without sight
we wander in the night

crashing into utopian contradictions
the magician made the Volkswagen disappear
what
where did it go

if everyone was a radical
and gazed into their telescope before declaring
I see nothing
then there would have to be a counterrevolution art
critic who would stand up
yelling crucify him

crucify her
crucify them all
and burn down the galleries
we don't want any more art
we're sick of it
it tells us nothing
nothing

go home to your townhouse in the ghetto
burn your toast
and spread some fig jam on it
eat and be happy
tomorrow your hell starts anew
oh my what shall we do
what terror awaits us

the past is a burden
it scorches the soul
demanding a ransom for silence

we must free ourselves from others expectations
but how can we be free when love puts us in chains
and our lovers demand we love them
perception grinds us into the ground
teaching us to view everything from an angle
inconsistent with reality

we are all refugees
we have no real home
our families leave us for greener pastures

abandoning us and leaving us penniless and sad
small wonder that we are depressed and lonely
trying to find friends that don't abuse us
or hold us hostage with their charms
creating fugitives that hide in dark places
rummaging around for spiritual food
and trinkets to amuse ourselves
calling out to the psychologists to save us

our lives are a mockery to institutionalized anarchy
we celebrate being out of control
believing ourselves to be progressive as we burn our
rulebooks

burning our bibles and
robbing our piggybanks
ripping our jeans
and spraypainting our sneakers
we struggle to identify who we've become
as an apocalypse is descending upon us

in its shadows we create new art
writing graffiti on our sidewalks
whilst our leaders rape the next generation
ambushing them in their sleep